For Halherein

May all your stories
have happy endings

love & blessings

i

Who Do You Think You Are?

by:
Rick Nichols

The
Crane's Nest
Books

Published by:
The Crane's Nest, a division of Health Horizons.
P.O. Box 1081
Bonsall, California, 92003
    (800) 969–4584

ISBN: 978-1-893705-09-8

Gift/Inspirational/Self-help

Cover and interior design by Rick Nichols
Illustrations by Greg High, www.greghigh.com
Interior Layout by Kera McHugh, www.time4somethingelse.com

Photography:
    www.shutterstock.com
    www.nasa.gov

The information in this book is designed to impart information to help individuals in
making positive changes in their lives. The ideas presented are not meant to substitute for
medical care or psychological assistance.

www.eagerlet.com

For Ginny with love

There are many beautiful and deeply spiritual temples around the world that through years of vandalism and neglect have been lost to the weeds; the overgrowth has become so thick that it is impossible to see the splendor within.

I do not know if you ever discovered this richness about yourself in your lifetime mom or if you just lost sight of it early on, but after all these years I have finally stumbled onto it.

I now know who you are; you are my hero.

Thank you for your selfless sacrifice in raising your family through very difficult times.

I love you,
Rick

A Heartfelt Gift for You

To: _____

From: _____

_____
_____
_____
_____

Gratitude

I would like to take this opportunity to thank all the people who have played a role, in one way or another, as mentors to me through the years. Whether or not you knew you were my mentor and whether or not you were gentle and patient, you provided important stepping-stones along the path. I am deeply grateful to you all. Thank you Kera McHugh for your patience as you tirelessly assembled these ever-changing words and pictures into a format acceptable by the demanding world of book manufacturing; you are a mountain of tolerance (most days). A special thanks to Christy Dickson, not only for your last-minute editorial services but also for unwittingly inspiring me to raise the story to a higher level than it might have been otherwise. Now to the fondest mentor of all, my wife and friend, Patricia. If I begin listing all the things about you that I am grateful for, this book would grow enormously and still fall sadly short of expressing the depth of my gratitude. So I will simply say thank you for all you are and all you do, I love you.

Finally, to all the Heal Your Life® teachers and life coaches around the world that Patricia and I have had the privilege to train over the years: we learn as we teach, and so thank you for all you have taught me as my students. Thanks also for the much needed work you are doing as you inspire people to the discovery of who they really are, which makes it easy for them to more fully love and appreciate themselves.

Table of Contents

Who Do *You* Think You Are?

Foreword

Who do you think you are, and why does it matter? A great philosopher offers deep insight on this question below ...

How can you get very far,

If you don't know Who You Are?

How can you do what you ought,

If you don't know What You've Got?

And if you don't know Which to Do

Of all the things in front of you,

Then what you'll have

When you are through

Is just a mess without a clue

Of all the best that can come true

If you know What and Which and Who

~ W. T. Pooh

Prologue

As the result of a seemingly innocent act of mischief on the part of the farmer's son, a magnificent creature intended for life in the wild high country is born into a family of turkeys on a small farm…

Part 1

Who Am I?

*O*nce, in a certain barnyard, at a certain time, there was born to a certain mother turkey six baby turkeys. All of the barnyard creatures came to the turkey pen to celebrate with Mother Turkey and to meet the new feathered members of their community.

Mother Turkey welcomed them all. It was a time of excitement and of, well, some curiosity.

"Oh!" the animals exclaimed. "Look at them! Three beautiful girls and two wonderful boys! And over there! Oh my! What is that? Is it a boy or a girl? Is it even a turkey at all?"

Mother Turkey protectively tucked the sixth and very odd-looking newborn under her wing, saying, "I know he's a little different from the others, but he'll grow into himself. Yes, yes, yes. I'm sure he will. He'll be just fine."

All the barnyard creatures nodded tentatively and agreed.

"Yes," they cackled and snorted and clucked. "Of course! You're right, dear. He'll . . . um . . . be just fine. Yes, just fine."

As they left the turkey pen, however, they were whispering to each other about this peculiar little bird.

"What an odd little fellow," they all said, shaking their heads. "Odd indeed."

Now, it would come to pass that Mother Turkey named her curious offspring Eagerlet because of his overly eager approach to almost everything. Eagerlet was different from the others. More than just in physical appearance, he was different at the level of his soul in ways that he could not even hope to understand from his current perspective. While his brothers and sisters were quite content to stumble about the barnyard, eating cracked corn and lying around in the dirt, he felt a call from deep in the fabric of his being, a powerful need to stretch his long, scrawny wings and fly far beyond the boundaries of the farm. He was always daydreaming about flying to the top—yes, to the top—of the barn, where he might perch upon the weathervane and finally see past the tidy little barn fences that made up this small world. Eagerlet dreamed of playing among the clouds, something a turkey would never imagine.

By and by, the older turkeys got together and agreed that if Eagerlet couldn't act more like a turkey, he was never going to fit in. They elected one of their elders to tell him so.

Eagerlet nodded politely and promised the elder that he would try harder. And he did; but for some reason, he just couldn't make himself into a turkey, no matter how hard he tried. He wasn't quite sure what to do, but after observing turkeys for a long time, he began to wonder why he would even want to be like a turkey. They pecked their corn and seemed quite satisfied with just lumbering about in the barnyard. Turkeys were obviously not dreamers.

Eagerlet had noticed a family of feathered creatures living across the barnyard. They seemed a little more like him. They were more active and didn't stumble and bumble around so much. Most importantly, they didn't make silly gobbling noises that turkeys were so fond of doing all day long. Aware that the farmer's son loved to play tricks on the animals, Eagerlet surmised that the son might have moved an egg from the chicken coop to the turkey pen resulting in this disaster.

"That must be it," he said to himself. "I was born into the wrong family!" With that, he promptly strolled across the barnyard and proudly took up residence with the chickens.

The chickens welcomed him at first, but it wasn't long before Rooster approached him and said, "You don't seem much like a chicken to me at all. You certainly don't act like a chicken. In fact, you look less like a chicken every day. If you expect to fit in with us, you're going to have to somehow make yourself into a chicken."

Eagerlet hung his head in shame and confusion, promising Rooster that he would try harder.

Rooster told Eagerlet that, if he expected to be a successful chicken, he would have to scratch for food and take it away from others in order to be sure to have enough for himself. Rooster also instructed him to constantly squawk and pick at the others in order to establish and maintain his superiority over them.

As promised, Eagerlet faithfully tried to do all of these things, but his heart just wasn't in them. He wasn't comfortable with this odd way of living. Deep within his soul he knew there was a much better way to live, and that somehow, he had to find out who and what he really was. Only then would he know where he belonged.

Taking a long look at the barnyard and the creatures that lived in it, Eagerlet decided it wasn't the place for him. It was so confining, so limited, and all barnyard creatures were hopelessly dependent upon others to provide for their needs. He, on the other hand, sensed a powerful yearning for freedom and independence. But what was he to do? Where was he to go? He felt lost and alone—afraid he might never find a place where he could fit in and be accepted.

There was one last feathered family on the farm that Eagerlet had not yet tried. They were very different in appearance from the all the others, mostly owing to the look of their beaks and feet. Their beaks were flat, wide, and long, bright orange in color, and emitted strange clucking and quacking noises. Eagerlet had, of course, never seen his own face but thought if he had a beak as long and bright as they had, he would surely be able to see the distant end of it. He had seen his feet, however, and they did seem similar in appearance to the other birds around the farm, with the one exception of this last family. Their feet were as orange as their beaks, and the area between each claw was filled with a thin skin of some kind. Eagerlet had often thought this a rather clumsy arrangement and figured it must be the reason for the way they sort of waddled from side to side as they moved about the barnyard. Unlike some of the other feathered families on the farm, this one did seem very pleasant and harmonious in the way they related amongst themselves, as well as with all the inhabitants of the farm.

Eagerlet gathered his courage and decided to risk yet another rejection in order to discover if this family is where he belonged. With soaring hope and high expectations, he bravely fell in behind the last of five ducklings as they trudged along behind their mother in a march across the grassy pasture.

Old Father Duck had been perched on a rock keeping a watchful eye out for foxes and other possible hazards when he realized a disaster was about to take place. Looking directly at Eagerlet, he gently said, "Eh-hem.

If you don't mind my saying so I don't think this is going to work out very well for you."

Eagerlet glanced timidly toward the old duck, trying to avoid eye contact, and asked, "No? Why not?"

"They're going for a swim in the old pond," replied Father Duck. "Please don't be offended, but I just don't think you're built for it."

"Built for what?" asked Eagerlet.

"For swimming. Little fellow, your body is simply not designed for swimming, and unless I've totally missed my guess, what your body is designed for is flying—flying very high," the old duck said. "Look at the difference in our feet and wings," he continued, pointing at his feet. "My webbed feet are made to help me glide easily through the water, and your long wings are to help you glide through the air."

Eagerlet stopped walking, sat down in the grass, and said, "Oh," unable to hide his disappointment.

"Come over here, and sit down for a moment," urged Father Duck. "I'd like to tell you a story."

Eagerlet stood up and forced himself to walk over to the rock as the old Duck suggested.

"You see, we're a family of ducks, and the nature of ducks is to swim. I don't know what family of creatures you are from, but I have heard stories— stories that have been passed down by word of mouth from ancestors of long ago that migrated here from the far north.

The stories tell of great, beautiful, and powerful creatures that live in high country and spend their days gliding above the landscape, watching over the earth and all its creatures. I think you may be descended from these magnificent creatures. I also believe it is time, Eagerlet, for you to leave the farm and seek the nature of who you are, what comes naturally to you, and how you can best serve the world.

Part 2

The Divine Cocoon

Confused and a bit ashamed
of not being able to measure up
to the expectations of all the other
farm creatures, Eagerlet
hung his head and
wandered into
the forest,
leaving the
barnyard
forever.

As it happened, Father Duck's sage advice for Eagerlet to strike out on his own seemed to be poorly timed. Great, dark clouds were gathering on the horizon as snow began to fall and a deep, ominous chill wrapped its freezing fingers about his young and fragile body.

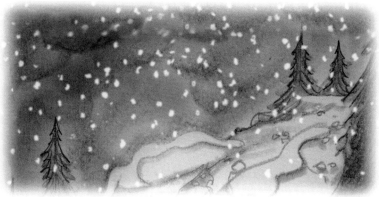

An un-seen and silent force of nature watches over the universe. Unknown to Eagerlet, this "Great One", had been with him all along, and had gently drawn him to a modest cave on the edge of the forest, where he might find safe haven in the rapidly approaching dark, cold, and lonely days.

Deep within the cave, the frozen grip of winter embraced Eagerlet with a bitter chill. Alone in the dark, he huddled close to the floor, shivering in the cold.

"What will become of me?" he asked himself as his consciousness slipped slowly, slowly away.

In time, Eagerlet awoke. He found himself still alone in the dark, but he was somehow warm and comfortable, as if something had wrapped itself around him. He couldn't imagine what this strange "something" might be, but he felt grateful nevertheless. He sensed that it was concealing him from the frozen drafts, which were moving silently through the cave in search of his otherwise vulnerable body.

Feeling quite hungry, Eagerlet imagined that even cracked corn and wheat chaff would look good about now. He sensed things moving about on the floor of the cave and picked up something with his beak. It was delicious! He didn't know what it was—probably a grub or a worm—but it was surely better than chicken feed! His aching hunger well-satisfied, Eagerlet drifted back into a deep and dreamless sleep.

This was the way of the winter for him: sleeping and eating—nothing else. . .

As Eagerlet slept, Mother Earth faithfully continued to turn round and round as she had for millions of years. Sun and Moon danced their special dance from north to south across the horizon, spinning days into nights, and nights into days until finally the darkness surrendered to the light. Sun sent its warm and brilliant rays directly into Eagerlet's sanctuary, awakening him to a new day, a new season, and an abundance of new opportunities.

Even though he had become comfortable in the cave, Eagerlet's intuition told him that it was time to go back into the world and search for his identity. He tried to stretch his legs and wings, but found to his alarm, that nothing except his head and neck were able to move.

"What is this?" he thought, as he pushed hard with his legs. It was as though he were wrapped in a cocoon of some kind. Fear flooded Eagerlet as he slowly realized his very life depended upon pushing through the confining grip of this thing that had wrapped itself around him through the winter.

He began to scratch with his claws and push with his legs. He pushed harder and harder until finally one little claw broke through the prison wall, followed closely by a scrawny little bird leg. After much struggle, the second leg broke through as well.

Now, to the wings, Eagerlet pushed and then pushed again, pushing harder and harder each time. Finally, the cocoon began to give and weaken bit by bit when all of a sudden—

22

Whamo....

Both wings popped out at the same time! He looked a bit like a winged turtle that was stuck to the floor of the cave.

Fighting to get his legs under him, Eagerlet eventually managed to stand up. There seemed to be something very heavy clinging to his back.

He stood in the cave swaying under what felt like the weight of the whole world on his back and shoulders. He could hardly bear the load. With Sun beaming brightly into the cave, he could see, for the first time, where he was and what his surroundings were like. He was in a cave filled with strange featherless birds, which were somehow perched upside down from the ceiling!

The floor of the cave and everything on it, including one turtle-like bird were covered with droppings of these odd creatures.

"Yuk! Yuk, yuk, yuk!"

"So this is what kept me from freezing during the winter!" he screeched, as he stood there wrapped in a cocoon of bat guano. Eagerlet shivered at the thought, sending guano flying across the cave. That was about the time that Grandfather Bat swooped down and landed on the floor in front of him.

Speaking in a soft and friendly voice, Grandfather Bat said, "Listen my friend, we've enjoyed your company all winter, but if you are going to stay here with us, you must behave more like a bat. At the very least, you'll have to learn to hang from the ceiling, and, well . . . need I say more?

Look at you. You're a mess."

This was a speech Eagerlet had heard before.
Having no desire to spend the rest of his days
upside-down in the dark, he thanked the bats for
their hospitality and headed off once again into the
forest on a quest for home and identity.

Part 3

Guidance From Above

*A*rriving at the edge of a sheer cliff and gazing over its precipice, Eagerlet suddenly felt an almost irresistible compulsion to leap out. "I cannot continue trying to make myself into something I am not." He thought, "I am who I am, and that is all I care to be—But what is that? And where do I belong?" At this moment, it seemed to Eagerlet as though he were destined to be a stranger to the whole world for the rest of his life.

Just about the time Eagerlet was going to give up on it all, he heard a piercing call from the heavens! This was a sound he had never heard before. Oddly, however, he felt in his heart that the voice was somehow familiar, a faded echo from some long, long time ago.

Eagerlet looked up to see two of the most wonderful creatures he had ever beheld. They seemed to be resting easily on the air, effortlessly slipping between the clouds and gliding across the sky.

"Wow!" he said, remembering his dreams of flying to the top of the weathervane on the roof of the barn. "If only I could be like that! If only I could soar among the clouds the way they do and see the world from such a height. Oh, life would be so grand! What freedom, what wonder they must experience up there."

As he watched the flight of the two splendid creatures, he was unaware that he was backing away from the edge of the cliff towards the forest.

An old owl, who had been watching from his perch in a pine tree, startled Eagerlet when he said,

"Who? Who? Who do you think you are?

What makes you think you could do such a thing? Look at yourself." He continued sternly, "You're too young and too inexperienced. Besides, those kinds of maneuvers take a lot of training. No, you just don't have it in you. You are not smart enough or good enough! Save yourself a lot of disappointment my friend, and just go back to where you came from."

Eagerlet looked at the old owl and remembered someone once telling him that owls were very wise. "Oh well." Eagerlet replied, his hopes fading away, "I guess you're right. I'm just a silly dreamer. Perhaps I should go back to the barnyard."

He shrugged his wings in resignation, hung his head once more, and started back towards the forest.

Ignoring the old owl's disheartening words, the great creatures in the bright blue sky called to Eagerlet a second time. He turned and looked up.

"I can do it," he said to himself with a mixture of stubbornness and confidence. "I know I can!"

He moved cautiously back towards the edge of the cliff, thinking he might be able to simply step off the edge, spread his wings, and fly. As he stood there, trying to work up his courage, a pair of nearby crows began to heckle Eagerlet.

"Caw! Caw! Caw! You can't do that. You've never done anything right in your entire life."

Watching the crows as they continued their intimidation and bullying, he hesitated for a moment, then started back towards to the forest.

But the two great creatures overhead were persistent. Again, they called to Eagerlet, their voices clear and strong. Again, Eagerlet looked up in awe of their flight.

"Yes I can!" he yelled as he raced towards the edge, preparing to make the leap. "I know I can."

A great South American toucan had been sunning himself on a nearby boulder enjoying the unfolding drama.

"No way, José!" Toucan admonished, in a disinterested tone.

"You'll never make it. You can't do such a thing. You don't have it in you!"

Eagerlet was on the verge of jumping when he heard Toucan's warning. Startled by the strange voice, he slammed on the brakes. Digging into the earth with his claws, he almost slipped over the edge, sending rocks and debris cascading downward.

He was more frightened and confused than ever. As tears began to form in his eyes, he blindly ran in shame, heading for the forest as fast as possible before anyone else could mock him.

He was almost to the tree line when, from on high, great calls came yet again. He stopped, turned, and looked up, still in awe of the creatures' majestic flight. Eagerlet focused on the edge of the cliff while the naysayers continued shouting their demoralizing words.

"Who do you think you are?"

"Caw! Caw! You can't do that!"

"No way, José. No way."

He covered his ears with his wings and he ran full out, screaming as loud as his voice would allow.

He screeched as he ran to the edge of the cliff and bravely leaped towards the heavens!

"I know I can fly!" He affirmed, "I know I can fly above the clouds! I am a great flyer!"

Eagerlet boldly spread his wings as far as he could, held his head high, and with great hope in his heart . . .

… fell like a rock.

He tumbled over and over, wrapping his wings
tightly around his head to try to protect himself
from the fall. He continued to fall upside-down,
downside-up. Faster and faster, deeper and deeper,
he plunged into the abyss.

As always, The Great One was with him, for slowly his senses faded away leaving only this simple instruction to fill his reality,

"Eagerlet, fly or die. You must choose now."

Was it a whispered voice? A feeling? A thought? He couldn't tell, but he knew it was a sensation he had never experienced before. Eagerlet was deeply aware that he had been given a choice to live or die in this moment, and whatever he chose would be the best choice for him. He wondered. . .

"What is it like being dead?"

A great sense of peace steadily overcame Eagerlet as he felt himself slowly slipping into a luminous void. For what seemed a long time he drifted deeper and deeper into the splendor of the colorless light, willingly and gently letting go of a life that never really seemed to welcome him anyway.

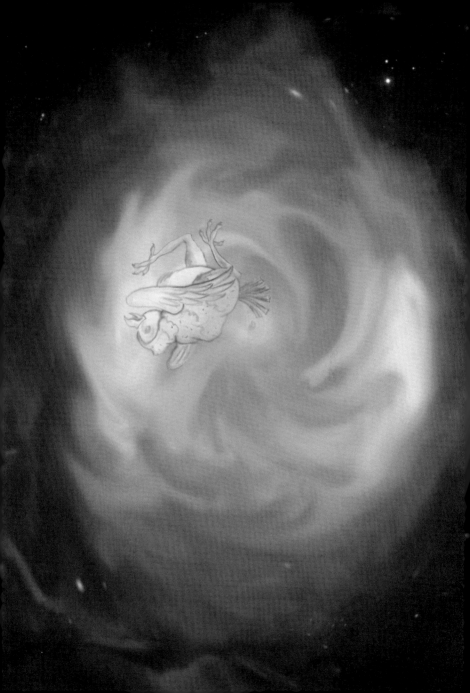

A formless energy—a single, focused thought—
suddenly sprang from the depths of his heart,
which forced a great deep breath that gave birth to
these words . . .

"FLY!
I choose to fly!"

As the power of Eagerlet's new affirmation echoed
through the valley, he confidently threw back his
head, spread his heavy wings once again and …

. . . slammed into the face of the cliff at full speed!

The impact of the collision threw him away from the cliff in a flurry of feathers and guano. The blow sent him into a state of semi-consciousness that caused his body to completely relax into the fall,

and...

Swishhh

"Whoa!" he screamed in amazement. "What's this? I'm flying! I'm really flying!"

Indeed, Eagerlet was flying, although not very well. His wings were untried, and he was still packing a heavy load of guano. The squawking gallery perched on the cliff above watched the scene with excitement and continued their mocking.

"Caw, caw! We told you so. We knew you couldn't fly! You should mind your elders!"

"No way, José. Adios! See you in that Great Forest in the Sky some day."

All Eagerlet wanted to do was escape the annoying hoots, squeaks, and squawks of these discouraging creatures. He pushed hard with his wings—once, twice, thrice—and then again. With each powerful thrust of his wings, more and more guano fell away, and he rose higher in the air. The two great birds above saw that he had made a bold commitment and was giving it the best he had. They also saw that he was struggling with his untrained talents; so, they swooped down to help. They flanked him on the right and left and gently escorted him to a warm thermal of air rising from the canyon floor. As the three of them rode the thermal, slowly rising higher and higher towards the clouds, the one on the right offered encouragement and hope.

"You can do it!" he said. "Say it! Say, I can fly so high!"

"I can fly so high!" replied Eagerlet, unable to contain his enthusiasm.

"Your wings are so powerful!" said the one on the right. "Say, my wings are so powerful. Say it now!"

"My wings are soooo powerful!" came the instant response.

"Is that good?" asked the one on the right, "or is that very good?"

"Oh, that's very good, all right!" Eagerlet agreed. "Very, very good."

The one on the left said, "Watch me. You can learn from me. Just do what I do." Up and up they went, all the way to the clouds and beyond. All day they soared through the heavens. The great teachers taught Eagerlet to dive, to swoop, to bank, and to turn. They taught him to fly so high that he could see where the ocean met the shore and beyond. Most important however, they taught him to ride the ever-changing winds and let their natural movement carry him effortlessly wherever he wanted to go. The one on the right constantly offered motivation and inspiration, while the one on the left demonstrated skill and technique.

Part 4

Self-discovery

As Sun slowly sank deeply into the distant ocean, they gently glided back to earth, coming to rest on the branch of a grand old tree that hung out over a clear mountain lake. This was one of those rare lakes of seemingly infinite clarity and depth—a lake of primordial wisdom, reflecting the moon, the stars, and an infinite universe. If anyone were to be still and look deeply—very deeply—into these sacred waters, he would surely find himself within.

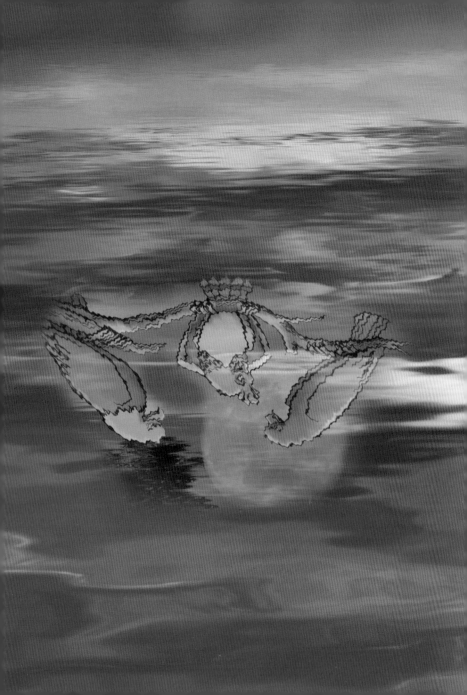

$\mathcal{E}$agerlet felt a sudden suffocating fear that these glorious birds would turn away from him as so many others had before. A great wave of loneliness swept over him as he gazed transfixed by the images in the lake. He felt as if the waters were drawing him into their deep, dark, and silent abyss. Panic began to creep into his consciousness producing a strong desire to claw his way back to the surface…

"Be still Eagerlet." Came a gentle voice, seeming to rise from the water,

"Be still and know you are safe." The voice is not *from* the water, Eagerlet thought, it *is* the water.

"You are never alone Eagerlet. Be still—allow the waters to purify, cleanse and heal.

"Allow, allow, allow. Allow your sacred inner light to fill the void and illuminate the world."

There in the dark well of grief Eagerlet received the gift of grace. The grace of knowing that all beings are beautiful and acceptable, regardless of the color of their plumage, the shape of their body, or their ways of being in the world. The deep still waters brought a different reflection for Eagerlet to consider. This inward reflection reminded him of his past journey and of those he had met along the way.

The grace of forgiveness is the greatest of gifts from the well of grief if one is willing to dive deeply enough to harvest it from the rich soil of the bottom. As Eagerlet reviewed his experience of the cliff top and its nagging, discouraging naysayers, he suddenly saw them in a completely different way. Through the lens of forgiveness, Eagerlet was able to see that these fellow beings were simply acting out of their own deep fear, doubt and uncertainty. In this most sacred moment, the grace of forgiveness broke open Eagerlet's heart; it became clear that an attack of any kind is always a desperate cry for love, and that the beings of the cliff top as well as all beings of the world deserve compassion and understanding rather than anger and retaliation.

Eagerlet's many blessings played out in his mind one after the other. He felt a deep sense of love and gratitude for Mother Turkey who patiently nurtured him through the early weeks, and for Elder Turkey for gently pushing him out of a nest that through no fault of his own was not his proper home. He silently expressed appreciation for the blunt honesty of Rooster, which made him aware of his unique need for independence. The memory of Father Duck and his story suggesting the possibility of a greater destiny came to mind, renewing his vision for a bright future. Even the black, featherless birds in the cave held a warm and special place of gratitude in his heart for their, uh — rich contributions, which protected him from the freezing winter.

After what seemed like a very long journey, Eagerlet slowly regained a sense of his surroundings. Everything was exactly as before, except that his two companions were gone. Rather than the sense of abandonment and loneliness that he may have felt earlier, he now felt perfectly at ease, comfortable and safe as he sat there joyously full of aloneness in the fading light of day. In the deep recesses of his mind he heard what felt like haunting echoes of the old owls' voice as it questioned:

Who? Who?
Who do you think you are?

"I Am . . .

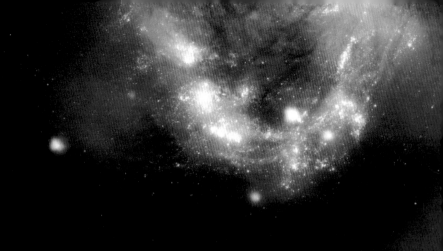

...I am a spark of

Divine creative potential

expressing uniquely as the one

who is known as Eagerlet."

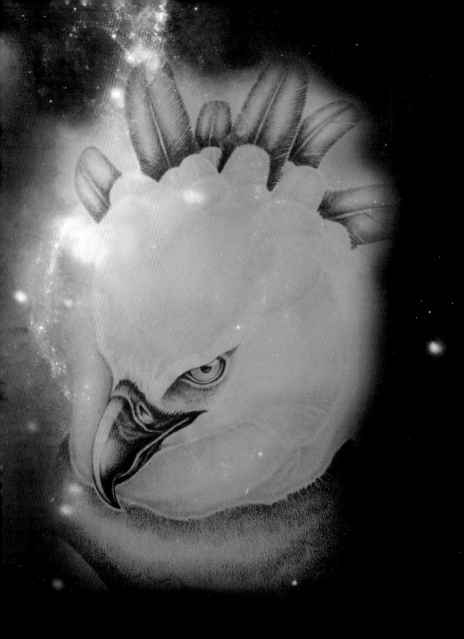

Epilogue

The little bird in the
heart's cage is putting out
it's head looking this way
and that way.

Is it safe to come out yet?

I choose to fly!

The
Beginning...

About the Author

Rick Nichols, a partner in Heart Inspired Presentations, LLC and an expert on Human Potential, is a writer, storyteller, and international speaker.

With his inspirational, warm, and humorous style Rick has captivated audiences around the world. He is a speaker of many facets: a storyteller, poet, and philosopher, as well as a teacher and student of life.

Never having known his biological father, Rick's destiny was to be raised by a pair of alcoholic combatants in a domestic war zone along with five siblings. Because of this and a "learning disability," he often felt like a misfit in a strange world. The rich diversity of Rick's salt and pepper background is sprinkled throughout his presentations. He has experienced the highs and lows of life, learned how to make the best of it, and is willing to intimately share it all with his audiences.

About the Artist

Greg High is a Southern California freelance artist-painter-illustrator.

With a couple degrees in fine art painting, Greg left the midwest in the 70's to seek the "good life" of Southern California. Scrounging for art assignments in San Diego, Greg took up with some multimedia producers, film directors and animators and began doing everything from conceptual storyboards to final production art, happy to be paid in sunshine dollars. During an ensuing successful career of over thirty-five years, Greg has produced thousands of artworks for a very diverse clientele (www.greghigh.com).

Today Greg continues to create art, illustrations and storyboards for special projects like Rick Nichols' inspirational "Who Do You Think You Are?" When not "making a living," Greg can be found in one of his home studios seeking the true Self through fine art painting, music composition and philosophic wonderings ... a life's work of art.

Through our company,
Heart Inspired Presentations, LLC,
we offer a variety of powerful programs
and products for personal growth.

For a current schedule and to see all of our products, please visit www.heartinspired.com. We are available to travel to your group for presentations.

Workshops, keynotes, and seminars include:
   Who Do You Think You Are?
   Heal Your Life® Workshop Leader Training
   A Return to Oz: Adventure of Self-Discovery
   Stress Management
   Success Strategies for Women on the Go
   The Magic of Believing in Yourself

Contact us at (800) 969-4584 or (760) 728-8783 or write to P.O. Box 1081, Bonsall, CA 92003.

E-mail:
   rick@heartinspired.com
   patricia@heartinspired.com

Find us online:
   www.facebook.com/rick.patricia
   www.facebook.com/patricia.crane
   www.youtube.com/healyourlife

Visit us our websites

www.HeartInspired.com
Our flagship web site and the hub for all the sites listed below. From here, you can learn all about us and what we offer that will be of value to you.

www.Eagerlet.com
Take a journey of discovery into who you really are.

www.HealYourLifeTraining.com
Learn how to assist others in their growth and enhance your own personal growth.

www.OrderingFromtheCosmicKitchen.com
Learn how to create and use powerful affirmations to improve your life in every way

www.MessagesFromTheAngels.com
Angels are the part of God that appear to us on earth in a way we can understand. Take a moment for communion with the angels. They will inspire you with a renewed faith that all is well.

www.TakingABreather.com
Relax and enjoy the peace and beauty of nature, music and art through a peaceful video presentation and learn simple techniques for managing stress.

www.ChangeInsideOut.com
Take our online courses for just one easy, affordable lifetime membership fee.